MW01675789

A NORWEGIAN GIFT OF LOVE

A MINNESOTA LAKES ROMANCE NOVELETTE

ROSE MARIE MEUWISSEN

Rose Marie Meuwissen

A NORWEGIAN GIFT OF LOVE

BY

Rose Marie Meuwissen

A Norwegian Gift of Love

Digital/Print Edition

https://www.rosemariemeuwissen.com

Print ISBN: 978-1-954030-01-5
Published in the United States of America
Nordic Publishing
Edited by Leanore Elliot
Cover Design by Rose Marie Meuwissen

nordic
PUBLISHING

Created with Vellum

To my dad, Sverre Waagen, who after much persuasion, agreed to order a bunad for me from the Husfliden in Bergen, Norway as a birthday gift. He was born in Gursken, Norway and their bunad is the Sunnmøre from the Møre Og Romsdal area. Unfortunately, or fortunately, depending on how you look at it, I have two sisters so he was obligated to buy three bunads. Also, to my mother who ordered the hand-made bunad blouse from Sue Sutherland's Bunad Buttiken in Ely, Minnesota and purchased the sølje pins to complete my bunad. This Norwegian gift of love from my parents, my bunad, is a gift I will enjoy and treasure my entire life.

A MINNESOTA LAKES ROMANCE NOVELETTE

Lake Harriet

A NORWEGIAN GIFT OF LOVE

After her grandfather, Ole Thorson, died, Sonja embraces her Norwegian heritage, its traditions, and one hot photographer from Viking Magazine.

Would her inheritance include a Nordic boyfriend?

MINNESOTA LAKES

Land of 10,000 Lakes

A NORWEGIAN GIFT OF LOVE

BY

Rose Marie Meuwissen

CHAPTER 1

Bells chimed throughout her apartment, as she made her way to the door.

"Good morning, ma'am, delivery for Sonja Thorson Miller," a man announced immediately when she poked her head through the slight opening of her front door. She accepted the proffered clipboard and signed her name, stating she'd received the package.

Sonja saw the Norwegian postage stamps and knew immediately what was inside. She opened the large box and carefully took out the hand-sewn Sunnmøre bunad, which was a Norwegian traditional folk costume. Apparently, the pictures hadn't done it justice, as it was absolutely the most beautiful dress she'd ever seen with its red floral stitching on black wool fabric. The attention to detail and stitching done by skilled and experienced hands was incredible. Her only fear about ordering the bunad online from the *Husfliden* store in Oslo was that it wouldn't fit when she got it. She walked into her bedroom and gently spread out the blouse and the bunad, with its sleeveless bodice type vest attached to a full-length black skirt, on the bed. Quickly, she removed her jeans and shirt, then put the delicately embroidered white blouse on first and then slipped the bunad over her head.

Relief spread over her face as she fastened together the ornate pewter hooks. It fit perfectly. She stood in front of the mirror, looking at her reflection. Her long blonde hair fell in curls over her shoulders, highlighting her petite slender figure as her blue eyes sparkled back at her. The picture it portrayed was definitely like a page out of a history book.

Mom, I hope you can see this. I know you would be proud to see me in this bunad from Norway, representing your ancestry.

After she gently took the bunad off and hung it on a heavy-duty hanger, she lovingly put it away in her closet.

She called her dad to let him know it had arrived. He had been unenthused when she told him she was ordering the bunad. Though, to her surprise, he said he knew about them, because her mother had often talked about the traditional folk costumes while she was still alive.

"Dad, the bunad arrived today and it is so beautiful. Can you come over to see it?" she asked.

"Sure, Sonja. I'll stop by after work tonight. I have a gift for you, too. I'll bring it along."

"Dad, you know you don't have to buy me things."

"I know I don't have to. Gotta go. See you tonight."

Sonja didn't have a clue what her dad had bought for her, since it wasn't something he usually did. She tapped her computer, bringing it to life again, and went back to work, setting up advertising pages for her clients on their websites and sending emails out to their customer lists.

At seven, her doorbell rang. Her dad, Karl, smiled brightly as she opened the door.

She leaned in to casually hug him, as he had never been the touchy feely type of guy. "Good to see you, Dad."

"It's been a busy day today, how was yours?" he asked as he walked inside carrying a small gift bag.

"Hectic as usual with all the normal deadlines for a Friday."

"So, where is this bunad you ordered?" he asked.

"In my bedroom, I'll get it." Sonja started to leave the room.

"Can you model it for me? I'd like to see it on you," Karl requested with a huge smile for his daughter.

"Sure, have a seat. It'll take a few minutes to put it on." Sonja grinned as she walked away. *He wants to see it on me!* She hadn't thought he would even want to see it, much less have her model it. Well, she couldn't show it to her mother or her grandparents, so she would be more than happy to show it to her father.

"Here it is," she said as she twirled around so the full skirt could be seen in all its glory. "So, what do you think?"

"You look beautiful. I know this would've made your mother very happy. Her Norwegian heritage always meant a lot to her." He picked up the gift bag and handed it to her.

She took it from him, wondering what could possibly be inside.

"Go ahead. Open it."

She set the bag down on the table and removed the tissue paper. Inside were two jewelry type boxes. She opened the first one to find a large Norwegian Solje pin. She only knew what it was because she recognized it from the *Husfliden*'s website from when she ordered the bunad. They were expensive, she knew that much.

"It's beautiful!" Sonja removed it from the box.

She fastened the two-inch silver pin adorned with hanging spoon-shaped silver pieces onto the front of her blouse, then reached inside to take the other gift out. This box was old, and when she opened it, she saw another, smaller Solje pin. She gently took it out, as it was obviously old and extremely delicate in nature.

"Dad. . ."

"It was your mother's." He stared at her shocked face.

"I never knew she had anything from Norway." She held it in her hand and was in awe of the pristine condition of the antique pin.

"She always wanted to get a bunad. In fact, the one you're wearing, the Sunnmøre bunad. But at the time, we couldn't afford it. One year, her mother—your grandmother, Gunhild, bought her this Solje pin for Christmas. She wore it proudly with her Norwegian sweater."

"Oh, Dad, I can't thank you enough for holding on to it all of these years and giving it to me. I will treasure this forever. It is like a double treasure since grandmother bought it for mother."

"The other one is from me. I bought it for you down at the Norwegian store, *Ingebretsen's,* on Lake Street in Minneapolis."

"And I will treasure this one, too, since you bought it for me." She attached the smaller older Solje pin below the new larger one.

"I'm so sorry, Sonja, that I deprived you of all of this. You could've spent time with your grandfather, but I was so wrapped up in my pain from losing your mother that for years I couldn't bring myself to see him. And by the time I came to terms with my loss, I felt I'd burned that bridge long before and was too afraid to try to mend it. I am so sorry, Sonja."

She reached out and hugged him. His body was shaking as he cried. "It's okay, Dad. I didn't understand when I was little, but I do understand now. There's nothing we can do about the past anymore, but we can make changes for the future."

CHAPTER 2

Sonja opened her laptop and searched on the internet for, *Ingebretsen's,* the store her dad had mentioned. They had a very informative website offering a huge selection of Norwegian and Scandinavian products for sale, as well as information about local Norwegian events.

It appeared there was still, even in this day and age, a Norwegian Lutheran Church, called *Mindekirken,* which held religious services and hosted events honoring the culture. The one celebration that caught her eye was the National Day of Norway, an official holiday in remembrance of their Constitution Day, observed on May 17th each year in Norway and America. It is commonly referred to as *Syttende Mai* and celebrated with a parade held in the streets surrounding the church. Everyone was encouraged to wear their bunads. Perfect, a place where she could finally wear the beautiful traditional folk costume. But, she felt a bit apprehensive about going alone and not knowing anyone. There was always her dad, though. Maybe now since he wanted to encourage her efforts to embrace her Norwegian heritage, he would accompany her.

"Dad, thanks for coming with me," Sonja said as he dropped her off at the door to the church and then went to find a parking place.

They found some of the last available seats in the balcony. She was amazed to see all the colorful and different bunads. From the *Husfliden's* website, she knew each region had their own specific bunad and they were all vastly different in style, but all were made with embroidery designs lovingly stitched by hand.

The church was overfilled, with people standing in the aisles and entrance foyer. Parts of the service were in English and some parts were in Norwegian. After the service, everyone lined up on the street outside the church to wait for the parade to begin.

She watched outside on the steps leading to the street, with her father, totally amazed at what she saw. There were a couple other women dressed in the same Sunnmøre bunad as hers. Everyone at the event seemed very friendly. A few people even came up to her and commented on how beautiful her bunad was. Some people carried Norway's flag and others displayed banners from the local Norwegian groups. She made a mental note of a couple names—Daughters of Norway and Sons of Norway—so she could look them up online later and possibly join their groups to learn more about her heritage.

Standing in the hot sun, Sonja felt the strong rays of heat piercing through the heavy 100% wool, floor-length bunad. Needless to say, the costume was warm, especially since it was almost seventy degrees, which was an unusually high temp for mid-May. Moving to a shady spot, she observed people taking photos of the parade and the many women walking in the street with their intriguing bunads.

One younger man in particular, probably close to her age, appeared to be a professional photographer and she couldn't help noticing he was extremely attractive. She'd anticipated the crowd to be older, and was actually surprised to see so many younger people, in their 20s or 30s, at the event. She wasn't sure where the idea came from, but she had thought it would be almost all older people—her grandfather's age or at least her dad's age.

After the parade, a Nordic band played in the church's parking lot and a light lunch could be purchased. Lunch seemed more American than anything else to her, as it was hot dogs, chips, and pop. *But then, what do I really know about Norwegian traditions? Absolutely nothing.* She wasn't really sure what to expect, but she'd heard a lot about Lutefisk being a Norwegian tradition.

"Having fun, Sonja?" her dad asked.

"I'm just trying to take it all in. It's actually a bit overwhelming." She continued observing the crowd.

Karl laughed. "You haven't seen anything yet. Just wait until you go to your first Lutefisk dinner."

"Pardon me, but I'd love to take your picture, if you don't mind," said a voice from behind her.

She turned around. It was the good-looking photographer she'd noticed earlier. His blond hair framed a chiseled, clean shaven face, and he stood tall, about six feet, his proud body trim and muscular. His deep blue eyes quickly scanned over her from head to toe, then lingered on her eyes.

"I'm Rolf Erickson, I'm taking pictures for *Viking* magazine." He continued staring at her.

Realizing she hadn't answered him, she said, "Sure."

After she posed so he could get a full shot, he took a few pictures. Then he checked the view screen on his camera to make sure he got some good ones.

He reached into his pocket, pulled out his business card,

and handed it to her. "If you send me your email, I can forward the pictures to you."

"Thanks, my name is Sonja Thorson Miller." She took the card from him.

Her dad walked over and shook Rolf's hand. "I'm her father, Karl Miller."

"Nice to meet you, sir," Rolf said and turned toward Sonja. "A few of the women dressed in bunads are going over to the Lake Harriet Bandshell to pose for some more pictures. If you're free and interested, I'd love to have you join them."

"That'd be great. This is her first time wearing hers and it sounds like the perfect opportunity to be a part of the *Syttende Mai* celebration," Karl answered.

Rolf looked toward Sonja for her response.

"I'd love to. Thanks for asking." Her face lit up as she locked eyes with his.

"Great. We're meeting over there at two. See you then." Rolf smiled and walked away, snapping pictures as he went.

"Well, he certainly seemed like a nice young man." Karl grinned.

"It's only for a picture, Dad. Not a date," Sonja teased.

"For now. But he's interested in you," Karl said firmly.

"How would you know?" Sonja asked, trying to keep a straight face.

"A dad can tell when a young buck is interested in his daughter. Trust me," Karl stated matter-of-factly.

"Whatever," Sonja quipped hoping he was right and walked toward the vendor booths to see what treasures were being offered.

CHAPTER 3

About one thirty, Sonja and her father pulled into the parking lot at the Lake Harriet Bandshell. Gazing out toward the lake, she couldn't help but remember the many times she'd walked around this lake with her dad as a child. Located in the heart of Minneapolis, the beautiful lake was surrounded by a path that beckoned to joggers, walkers, bikers, and skaters. She would have to make a point of coming down here again for a nice, long walk around the lake.

There were about ten other ladies waiting, each dressed in a different bunad. She joined them just as Rolf approached.

"Thank you all for coming. I think we'll get some great shots here that will work well for the article I'm doing for *Viking* magazine. First, I will take single shots of everyone in various poses and then we'll do some group shots," Rolf instructed the group, but his eyes were glued on Sonja.

She was assigned to the end slot, probably because she was last to arrive. Her dad just smiled an I-told-you-so look from a distance. The women waited patiently and went up one by one to have their pictures taken. Since it was a large stage, he moved agilely around them, snapping pictures from different angles. Finally, it was her turn. She walked up the stairs to the stage. To say she wasn't a little nervous would've been a lie because she'd never done any type of modeling before and felt just a bit self-conscious about the whole thing.

"You're doing great. How about a big smile?" Rolf coaxed.

Sonja smiled, simply because she couldn't help it. His grin was contagious and dazzling, nothing like hers, she was sure.

"Now, how about you think about your first kiss?" Rolf suggested.

He snapped away furiously as she thought about that kiss. Her response was instantaneous and without a care in the world about how her face portrayed the memory.

"Sonja, you can stay up there and let's have numbers eight and nine join her, please."

They came up and joined her on stage and he snapped away. Then the rest came up a couple at a time and soon everyone was on stage. They posed for many pictures before he was satisfied that he had enough shots.

"I can't thank you enough, ladies. Now, if you could all sign the release forms allowing me to use the pictures in the magazine and leave your email on the bottom of the form so I can share the pictures with you, we'll be finished." Rolf gave everyone a form, his hand lingering on Sonja's as he passed her the last one.

She picked up the pen he'd offered and began filling it out. The others finished, handed Rolf their forms, and left. He came over to stand by her since she was the only one still there. When she was done, she looked up to see he was staring intently at her. He made her feel nervous but at the same time her heart was beating madly in her chest.

She handed him the paper. "Thanks, it was fun. I'm excited to see the pictures."

"If you'd like, I would love to print some out for you. Maybe we could meet for coffee next week and I can bring some copies?"

"Sure," she said and couldn't help flashing him a big smile.

"Would the Starbucks at the Barnes and Noble in the Eden Prairie Mall work for you?"

"That's perfect. I live in Eden Prairie," she responded.

"What night works best for you?" he asked.

"How about Thursday at five thirty?" she suggested.

"Great. I'll send you an email this week to confirm." He watched as she looked over to where her dad was waiting patiently and watching them.

"I should go. My dad's waiting. See you Thursday." She extended her hand as her heart beat rapidly and a warm flush flowed through her body when they touched. Her hand lingered too long in his before she released it and walked away.

CHAPTER 4

On Thursday, she sat at a café table in the Barnes and Noble store waiting for Rolf to arrive. Meeting men always filled her with dread, causing her to arrive early. Mainly because she was so nervous about being late, she ultimately ended up being fifteen minutes early. The email he'd sent yesterday was nice, there wasn't anything to worry about. She just hadn't gone out with anyone for months. No wonder she was jittery. She hated first dates, but heck, this wasn't even a date. Actually, she wasn't entirely sure what it was. Then, he walked through the door and his face immediately lit up when he saw her.

"So good to see you again, Sonja." His eyes roamed over her in a speculative evaluation. "You look really good. Without the bunad, I mean." He must have noticed the puzzled look on her face. "Never mind, that didn't come out right."

"That's okay. Thanks. I think? It was a compliment, wasn't it?"

"Absolutely! Sorry, it's just that sometimes it's hard to tell what a woman really looks like with those big bunads covering them from head to toe… I think I should just shut up now." He set his bag on the table and sat down.

"I understand what you're saying. It's fine." She was definitely glad she'd worn her skintight jeans and a fitted sweater to show off her figure.

"Can I get you something to drink?" he asked.

"Sure. I'll come up too so you don't have to try and remember my complicated coffee drink." She laughed and followed him to the counter.

After they ordered, they sat down once again. Rolf took out the photos and handed them to her. "I think your pictures turned out really great. You are extremely photogenic."

She picked up the pictures and looked at them one by one. There were ten in all. She wasn't so sure she agreed with the part about her being photogenic, but they were all very good shots. It probably had more to do with that he was a really good photographer.

Rolf watched her intently as she studied the pictures. When their names were called, he got up to get their drinks. He set them down as she finished studying the last picture. "What do you think?"

"They do look good. I think it's because you are a talented photographer. I don't usually have my picture taken, but I do like these."

"You can keep them. I made these copies for you."

They both took sips of their drinks and didn't speak.

Rolf broke the silence. "I know this seems a little strange since we don't really know each other, so how about I go first. I grew up here in the Twin Cities, went to Chaska High School, and then Augsburg College. I have a degree in Photo Journalism. I freelance, work for *Viking m*agazine as well as have my own photography company online where I sell my photos. I'm half Norwegian on my father's side and have been attending Norwegian events since I was a little kid. I'm single, haven't been in a serious relationship for over three years."

"Wow. I totally know you now! But probably, not really. Okay, here's my story. I'm from Eden Prairie, went to Eden Prairie High School, and then attended Mankato State University. My degree is in Marketing and Advertising which I used to start my own company, SOMAR, where I do online marketing for small companies to get their names out in front of the public. The *Syttende Mai Parade* was the first Norwegian event I've attended, even though I'm also half Norwegian. I'm single and have only dated casually because I haven't met anyone I liked enough to have a serious relationship with."

"I think I'm in love. Want to get married?" Rolf joked.

"Oh, definitely. It must be one of those 'Love at First Sight' situations."

They both laughed.

"Okay, I have a question. Why haven't you been to any Norwegian events?" Rolf asked.

"Unfortunately, my mother was the one who was 100% Norwegian, but she was killed in a car accident when I was just five. My dad took it extremely hard and since her parents were everything Norwegian, which reminded him of my mother, he cut off all ties with them. So I was never able to learn about my heritage from them. Plus, they lived in Wisconsin so they weren't just down the street or anything like that," Sonja explained.

"I'm sorry you missed out on your Norwegian heritage growing up. It was a huge part of my life and put me where I am now. What made you finally reach out to come to the event?" Rolf asked.

"My grandfather died recently and in his will instructed me to purchase a bunad from the Ålesund area, where his parents were born, and to make plans to visit Norway. He left me the money to pay for all of it, of course. So I ordered the bunad online and searched the internet to find local events where I could possibly wear it," Sonja answered, summarizing the stipulations of the will.

"Your grandfather must've been heartbroken that he wasn't able to share his ancestry with you. But what a wonderful legacy to leave you in his will. The financial means that would allow you to explore your heritage, even after he was gone," Rolf said, offering encouragement.

"In a heartfelt letter given to me by his lawyer, he expressed regret that he hadn't been able to share his pride and love for Norway with me since we lived so far apart. I never realized how much I missed, and probably how much he missed not being able to share it with me while he was still alive, until I attended his funeral last March," Sonja admitted and her eyes became misty while she talked.

"So, do you know exactly where your relatives are over in Norway? Did he still have contact with them?" Rolf asked.

"Of that, I'm not sure. My grandmother died shortly after my mother's death years ago, so I don't really have much to go on. I did receive a box of keepsakes from my grandparent's estate. I was planning on going through them and possibly taking a genealogy class to do more research," Sonja offered and quickly brushed a tear away.

"The *Mindekirken* offers genealogy classes put on by the Norwegian Genealogy Association. I've wanted to take some of their classes for quite some time, to see how far back I can trace my family. I think they have one starting in June," Rolf offered.

"I would like to take that class, because if I'm going to Norway, it would be nice to know if I still have some relatives over there I could stop in to visit." Sonja smiled.

"I will check it out and email you the details," Rolf promised.

"Great! It would certainly be more fun to take a class with someone you know." Sonja's heart beat rapidly in her chest. Her attraction to Rolf was intense and the thought of getting to spend more time with him made her extremely happy.

"I've kept you talking for an hour now and you're probably starving. Let me buy you a sandwich. Then maybe we can continue our conversation for another hour?" Rolf asked as he watched for her response.

"I haven't had dinner yet, so a sandwich would be great. And then we can see where the conversation leads," she said as she smiled across at him.

CHAPTER 5

Rolf called her the next day to let her know where to register for the Genealogy class. Sign up was available on the *Mindekirken's* website.

Unfortunately, the following week, he needed to be in Moorhead for a photo shoot of the Hjemkomst Viking Ship and a Viking re-enactment festival, instead of spending more time with Sonja. While he was gone though, he called her almost every night and she found herself looking forward to the next time he would call.

On Saturday, she woke to a bright, sunny day with temps expected in the seventies. It would be a great day for a walk and to be outdoors, so she headed to Lake Harriet.

She paced herself so she could make it the whole way around the lake. When she finished, she sat down on a bench to rest and look out over the water. The lake was still cold from winter, but would be warming up a little more each day. Soon the beach would be full of people in their swimsuits, enjoying sunbathing and swimming. The gentle sound of waves rolling onto the beach filled the air.

It was a vastly different day from the cold and dreary day

of her grandfather's funeral in March, only a few months ago. The memory was vivid in her mind as she recalled the day.

Sitting in a pew at the front of the church, she'd reached into her purse to pull out another Kleenex to wipe the tears from her face. Tears that of their own accord continued to roll down her cheeks. Her grandfather, Ole Thorson, lay in a coffin at the front of the church while the pastor told wonderful stories about his life. A life she had not been a part of. Her mother, Greta Thorson Miller, died in a car crash twenty years ago when the car she was driving was struck broadside by a drunk driver. Miraculously the drunk driver survived. Unfortunately, her mother hadn't. She'd only been five years old at the time, so she remembered very little about her mother or her mother's family. Her dad, an insurance salesman from a stout German heritage, sat quietly beside her.

She'd listened intently to the stories about her grandfather's life, realizing it was most likely her last chance to get to know anything about him. After her mother died, her and her dad only went to visit her grandparents a few times because each time they'd visited, her father became extremely depressed knowing that the city of Stoughton was where the love of his live had grown up. He'd felt so much anger since his wife was no longer alive, but the drunk driver was still living and able to go on with his life.

Listening to the stories told by the pastor and other friends of Ole Thorson, she realized her grandfather had been a very likable person. Someone she would probably have enjoyed spending time with. But with her mother gone, the connection had been broken. She felt as if her heart had shattered into a million pieces while the last remnants of her mother slipped away.

Two of the hymns were sung in Norwegian at the Holy

Cross Lutheran Church in Stoughton, Wisconsin, and after the service, they followed the coffin to the cemetery next door.

Time seemed to stand still, but then she found herself walking slowly back to the church and descending the steps to the basement. Members of the church had set out photo boards filled with pictures of Ole and her grandmother, Gunhild, who had passed away shortly after her mother died, years ago. She'd taken pictures of each board, then went back to intently look at each picture board to take in as much as she could about her mother's life in the small city.

Shortly after she'd memorized the last picture, she'd snuck outside and strolled slowly toward the cemetery to her grandfather's grave.

She'd felt so empty inside and her heart was broken. Besides her father, who refused to talk about her mother or her family, Ole Thorson, a complete stranger to her, was the only other person who'd ever really known her mother.

She'd felt the tears forming in her eyes once again and voluntarily let them roll furiously down her cheeks. Those tears weren't for her mother or her grandfather. No, they were for her and all the memories she'd missed out on during her young life.

But today was a sunny day and so was her future outlook on life. She was pursuing her Norwegian heritage along with a hot Norwegian guy who made her feel wonderful with just the touch of his hand. A smile crossed her face as she got up to walk around the lake one more time.

CHAPTER 6

Two weeks later, Sonja walked into the *Mindekirken*'s basement for the genealogy class where she was meeting Rolf. They hadn't gotten together since their Starbuck's sort-of date, but had emailed multiple times a day and talked on the phone. He sent her links to interesting Norwegian articles he'd come across, which led to her frantically searching the internet to find things she could share.

That first day of class, she sat down next to Rolf who'd saved her a chair at his table. She was ecstatic to learn how to research her genealogy, and listened intently as the instructor gave the info they all would need to get started. She opened her laptop and began getting set up with a log in for the genealogy site.

In the back of the room was a table set up with Norwegian cookie treats, coffee and apple cider. The cone shaped Krumkake had become her favorite and she was eager to get the recipe so she could try making them.

The class went on for four weeks and she looked forward to each one, as with each week she came closer to finding her relatives in Norway. After each class, Sonja and Rolf would go grab a bite to eat and talk more about themselves and their dreams. And as each week went on, her feelings for Rolf grew stronger. After the last class, they went to Matt's Bar to celebrate with their famous burgers.

"Have you had any luck contacting some of the names you've found in the Ålesund area?" Rolf asked, while they waited for their burgers and fries.

"Just got one today from a cousin of my mother's. It was from one of her kids who is my age, Anna Lise, and she would love to meet a relative from America," Sonja proudly announced.

"That's wonderful. Are you planning on going to Norway this summer?" Rolf asked as the waitress brought their beers.

"I would like to, but I don't really want to go alone. I have a cousin, Marie, who lives in Dallas and another cousin, Gretta, who lives in Seattle. They also were in grandfather's will with the same stipulation to spend the money to purchase a bunad and travel to Ålesund, Norway. Their fathers, whom I've never met, were my mother's brothers who had moved away to Texas and Washington right out of high school. Unfortunately, I'm not so sure I want to go with them. I've never spent any time with them and really don't know them at all," Sonja confessed.

"I can understand that. Travelling with people can be difficult and if you don't even know them, it can be even worse. What about your dad? Would he go?" Rolf asked.

"I haven't asked him. Remember, he never wanted anything to do with the Norwegian stuff. So, I don't think he'd go." She'd thought about asking him but hadn't done it.

"You might want to check out Brekke Tours. They have multiple travel packages to Norway and then you would go with a group. You could always add on days to go on your own to visit your relatives." Rolf watched the conflicting emotions cross her face.

"That would probably be the best thing to do. I could check out their packages to find out the best one and then at least ask my cousins if they'd like to go."

After enjoying their burgers, Rolf walked Sonja to her car.

"Sonja, I like spending time with you. I know we've both been busy with our jobs lately, but I was thinking maybe we could go out this weekend. I heard about a new restaurant, *Valhalla,* near Stillwater that I'd love to take you to for dinner Saturday night."

She stared at Rolf. A guy she couldn't find anything about not to like, and who actually appeared slightly nervous while he waited for an answer. He made her feel so at ease and she loved the bond they'd formed searching the archives of Norway for distant relatives along with the emails and phone calls they'd shared. Nothing would make her happier than to spend more time with him because she knew Rolf was a guy she could easily fall for. She could only hope he felt the same.

"I'd like that. It sounds like a fun place," Sonja answered.

"Great! I'll call you tomorrow," he said.

And then, he leaned down and kissed her, first a light kiss on the lips which deepened and left her yearning for more. Sonja was sure she was in *Valhalla* at that very moment. But it was over way too quickly and she definitely wanted more. She could tell he was holding back and trying to be a gentleman, as he leaned back a little to gauge her reaction. Her eyes were filled with passion and she didn't try to hide it, but more of *Valhalla* was best left for another time. Besides a parking lot was not the place she wanted to pursue this fire burning between them and find out where it would lead. To his surprise and hers, she leaned into him and boldly kissed him, then backed away.

"I'd better get going. Talk to you tomorrow," she said and got into her car quickly before she changed her mind.

Sonja spent the next day searching the internet for package trips to Norway. She found Brekke Travel did have the best prices. In fact, they had a package that would work perfectly. She emailed the info to her cousins, along with her preferred dates of travel. At the last minute, she decided to send it to her dad, also. Although, she had no hopes that any of them would take her up on the offer to accompany her on the trip.

Before she knew, it was Saturday and she was dressing for her date with Rolf. Unsure what to wear, she stared into her closet. She finally picked a recently purchased t-shirt, printed with a replica of the Norwegian flag and a pair of skintight blue jeans to accentuate her trim body. He was picking her up soon so she quickly finished curling her hair and putting on her makeup.

She was excited to check out this new restaurant with a Norwegian theme. As they walked in, she observed the various different Viking shields adorning the walls and a table holding three Viking helmets with horns, placed on furs.

"Wow, this is really cool," she commented as they took their seats at the table.

They looked the menu over and made their choices for the waiter.

She ordered the meatballs and he ordered the cod basket, along with Valhalla's own home-brewed Viking ale.

"I have to say, I'm impressed with this place," Rolf said as they were leaving. "How is your trip planning going?"

"It looks like I will have to travel alone if I go. My cousins finally got back to me and said they weren't sure they could take time off from work this summer. "

"What about your dad? Did you ask him to go?"

"I sent him the info, but I didn't get a response yet." Sonja stopped walking when they reached his car and he opened the door for her to get in.

During the whole ride home, she was anticipating whether she would get another kiss. And, when he walked her up to her door, he took her in his arms and kissed her long and hard, leaving her breathless. She knew she wanted him but she wasn't sure how much further she wanted to go at this point. After a couple more long sensual kisses, he said goodnight and left. He hadn't pushed her and it was obvious he was taking his time, which was perfectly fine with her. But the other question she kept asking herself was if she should ask him to accompany her on the trip to Norway?

CHAPTER 7

Four weeks later, Sonja finished packing her suitcases for her two-week trip to Norway. Alone. No one had been able to go with her, so she had decided to go anyway. She'd never gotten up the courage to ask Rolf, even though their relationship had been moving along in the right direction. It just seemed a little odd to go on a trip with someone you'd only recently met and weren't sleeping with yet. Even though she knew they would get to that point soon.

Her dad was picking her up shortly to take her to the airport.

Sonja just finished lining her bags up at the door when he arrived.

"I think it takes great courage to go on an international trip alone. But no one should go alone, especially a young woman such as yourself," he said as he loaded her bags into the car.

"Dad…we talked about this and no one could go," Sonja replied.

"Well, not exactly. I decided your mother would never

forgive me if I let you go by yourself, so I'm going with you," he announced.

"I can't believe you didn't tell me before now." A huge smile spread across her face.

"I wasn't sure if I could get away, and then I wasn't sure I could get a ticket and still get on the tour until last week," Karl explained.

"Thank you, Daddy. I can't tell you how happy this makes me," she said and hugged him before getting into the car.

Minutes later, they arrived at the airport and made their way to the ticket counter for Icelandic Air located at the Minneapolis St. Paul Humphrey Terminal.

She couldn't believe her eyes. Standing in the corridor was Rolf, with a suitcase, walking toward her.

"Rolf, what are you doing here?" Her heart was pounding so hard in her chest and she felt lightheaded. *Was she really going to be able to share this trip to Norway with him?*

"Well, you know my relatives are in the Ålesund area, too. But the main reason was I wanted to experience this with you." He released the handle of his roller bag and set his backpack down on the floor.

Sonja let go of her bag, set her purse down and closed the distance between them. She wrapped her arms around his neck and kissed him like she never wanted to let him go. This was going to be the trip of a lifetime, and she couldn't wait to spend it with the two most important men in her life.

Rolf held Sonja tightly in his arms, returning her kisses, then he leaned back to look into her dazzling eyes. "My favorite saying is, 'This is the first day of the rest of your life,' and I'd like to make it the first day of the rest of our lives together."

Tears formed in Sonja's eyes. "I'd like that, too."

They heard someone coughing behind them. "May be a good thing I'm coming along to chaperone the four of you."

"Four?" Sonja asked.

"Yes, your cousins are meeting us in Oslo. They couldn't come for the whole time so they will be meeting up with us for the second week."

Sonja couldn't help the huge smile spreading across her face. She was positive this was the best day of her life, so far anyway. She was also sure her grandfather never expected his last will and testament would bring them all together. It was truly a Norwegian gift of love on his part. Not to mention, his gift had helped her find Rolf, who she was extremely positive would end up being a permanent part of her life.

This trip could very well end up being her very own *Nor (Norwegian)—way to Love!*

RECIPE

KRUMKAKE

Ingredients

- 1 Cup sugar
- ½ Cup butter melted
- ½ tsp nutmeg or cardamom
- 3 eggs beaten well, pale yellow
- ½ Cup whipping cream—whipped by hand
- 2 Cups flour

Beat eggs, add sugar, fold in whipped cream, then butter and nutmeg. Add flour sparingly.

Place a Tablespoon in the center of each patterned circle on the double electric Krumkake maker.

Check after a minute to see if golden, then remove one and roll around the Krumkake roller, then remove the second one and roll on the other Krumkake roller.

Repeat. Slide Krumkake off the roller and place in air tight container to store.

Serve plain or fill with whipped cream or flavored mousse.

ABOUT THE AUTHOR

ROSE MARIE MEUWISSEN

Rose Marie Meuwissen, a first-generation Norwegian American born and raised in Minnesota, always tries to incorporate her Norwegian heritage into her writing. After receiving a BA in Marketing from Concordia University, a Masters in Creative Writing from Hamline University soon followed. Minnesota is still where she calls home.

She has traveled around the world, including Scandinavia, but still has many places to see, enjoys attending Scandinavian events, writing conferences and is usually busy writing Minnesota Lakes Contemporary Romances, Viking Time Travel Romances or Norwegian Traditions Children's Books.

Visit her at www.rosemariemeuwissen.com or www.realnorwegianseatlutefisk.com.

NOVELS:

- ***Taking Chances***—a contemporary romance novel set in Minnesota and Arizona.
- ***Married by Saturday***—a contemporary romance novel set in Minnesota and Montana.
- ***Lucky Vegas***—a contemporary romance set in Minnesota and Las Vegas.
- ***Looking for Mr. Right***—a contemporary internet dating romance novel set on Prior Lake in Minnesota—***Coming soon!***

NOVELLAS:

- ***Annika—A Christmas Romance***—a contemporary romance set in Minnesota with a Nordic theme during the Christmas Holidays.
- ***Skol! Viking Blonde Ale***—a contemporary romance set in Minnesota at an Autumn festival complete with a fortune teller, ale and Vikings!
- ***Choosing to Live***—a Norwegian woman's journey during WWII to survive the Nazi Occupation of Norway—***Coming soon!***

MINNESOTA LAKES ROMANCE NOVELETTES:

- ***A Kiss Under the Northern Lights***—a Summer romance set in Ely, Minnesota on Big Lake.
- ***Dancing in the Moonlight***—a Summer romance set in Malmo, Minnesota on Mille Lacs Lake.
- ***Hot Summer Nights***—a Summer romance set in Prior Lake, Minnesota on Prior Lake.
- ***Railroad Ties***—an Autumn romance set in Two Harbors, Minnesota on Lake Superior.
- ***Blizzard of Love***—a Winter romance set in Lutsen, Minnesota on Lake Superior.
- ***A Norwegian Gift of Love***—a Spring romance set in Minneapolis, Minnesota on Lake Harriet.
- ***Old Yule Log Fires***—a Christmas romance set in Excelsior, Minnesota on Lake Minnetonka.
- ***A Date for Valentine's Day***—a Valentine romance set in Minnetonka Beach, Minnesota at the Lafayette Country Club on Lake Minnetonka.
- ***Dance of Love***—a Fall Festival romance set at the Renaissance Fair in Shakopee, Minnesota.

CHILDREN'S BOOKS—REAL NORWEGIAN'S SERIES:

- ***Real Norwegians Eat Lutefisk***—a Children's book about the tradition of Lutefisk presented in both English and Norwegian.
- ***Real Norwegians Eat Rømmegrøt***—the second Children's book in the series about the tradition of Rømmegrøt presented in both English and Norwegian.
- ***Real Norwegians Eat Lefse***—the third Children's book in the series about the tradition of Lefse presented in both English and Norwegian.
- ***Real Norwegians Eat Krumkake***—the fourth Children's book in the series about the tradition of Krumkake presented in both English and Norwegian—***Coming next!***

MICRO-MINI NOVELETTE—COMING SOON!

- ***Christmas Notes***—a collection of Christmas prose poems to warm the heart during the Christmas season.

CONTINUE READING FOR A PREVIEW OF:

SKOL! VIKING BLONDE ALE

SKOL! VIKING BLONDE ALE

FORTUNES, LOVE & FATE SERIES

Print Edition

ISBN 978-0-9903788-3-9

Published in the United States of America
Nordic Publishing LLC
Cover Design by Raine English

SKOL! VIKING BLONDE ALE

FORTUNES, LOVE & FATE SERIES

Inga was living the dream, planning events for her own company, Unique Events, but she still hadn't found a guy who could be 'The One' for her. She never would've believed a fortune from a gypsy fortune teller promising her a 'love that surpasses time' could come true.

Erik moved from Norway to Minnesota to expand his Nordic Brewing company in the U. S. He'd promised himself to devote all his time to the business, but how was he to know that an unknown force of fate would introduce him to a woman he couldn't walk away from?

Their attraction could not be denied because ultimately, they were destined to be together. But could the Atlantic Ocean keep them apart? Would that even be possible if they were truly soul mates?

INGA'S FORTUNE:

Someone from your past will reappear in your life.
Your true soul mate.
With him, you will experience a love that surpasses time.

PROLOGUE

James J. Hill Days in Wayzata on Lake Minnetonka
September

Inga pulled into the back-parking lot of Main Street Books at six. She couldn't believe it wasn't later. Friday night rush hour traffic on the 494 Freeway was bumper to bumper all the way from Eden Prairie to Wayzata. The weather was still holding its summer like temps and true Minnesotans would never pass up a beautiful autumn weekend to go up North to their cabins one last time before winter arrived. Today was the James J. Hill Days celebration in Wayzata and the main street was packed with people as she made her way into the book store to find her *Romancing the Lakes of Minnesota* book club. This month instead of their regular meeting, they planned to enjoy walking around and checking out the celebration. Probably was a good call, she thought, since it would've been difficult to hold their meeting in the crowded book store and the activity outside would've been immensely distracting.

"Am I the last one to arrive?" Inga asked as she approached the book club group standing in front of the latest arrival shelf where the romance section was located.

"Bet the traffic was awful," Nora stated.

"Ready, to brave the crowds?" Katie asked.

"I'm hungry and thirsty, let's go!" Violet said.

Inga nodded in agreement and followed the group out the door to Main Street. They made their way down the street stopping at booths to look at the novelties for sale until finally, they stopped at the end of the street where the most unusual trailer was parked. The sign above the open door read, 'Fortune Teller'. It appeared to be Vintage, but these days they could make anything look old, even if it was new. Although, she had to admit, she'd never seen anything like it before, even though she'd been to many events. After all, she was an event planner. Intrigued was putting it mildly. Unfortunately, there was no stopping her curiosity. So, she entered the trailer.

"Come in, please," a very thickly accented voice beckoned from inside the trailer.

"Hello." Inga ducked and stepped into the trailer, taking in all the antiques and draped surroundings.

"Take a seat," the lady in gypsy like garb directed. "Let me see what your life has in store for you."

Inga didn't believe in fortune telling, at least she didn't think she did, but what could it possibly hurt to oblige the lady. It might be worth a laugh later, so she sat down on the partially pulled out chair at the table.

The fortune teller took the seat across from Inga and reached for her hand.

Slowly, Inga extended her hand. When their hands touched, Inga felt a strange sensation flow through her entire body, almost like a spark of electricity. It only lasted a few seconds and then was gone. She had no idea what it was or what caused it, but she finally relaxed.

The woman's face seemed deep in thought and completely fixated on her hand. "You are a very special lady. Very strong and independent. I see happiness in your future."

"Do you see a man?" Inga wasn't sure why'd she'd asked that particular question.

"Yes." The woman continued staring at her hand. "A very handsome man."

"Well, there certainly are enough good-looking men around. What I need is one that is interested in me long enough to stick around for a while."

"You have not met '*The One*' yet."

"When? When will it happen? I'm getting really tired of waiting around for him."

"Soon."

"So, is that my fortune?"

"No." The woman hesitated, then picked up a piece of paper and wrote a few lines down on it. She handed it to Inga. "This is your fortune: ***Someone from your past will reappear in your life. Your true soul mate. With him, you will experience a love that surpasses time.***"

"Great. But I'm sorry, I don't believe in magic."

"That's okay you don't have to believe. It will happen anyway."

Their eyes locked for a moment.

Inga got up to leave. "How much do I owe you?" Inga asked.

"For you, no charge. I've been waiting for you."

"I don't understand."

The fortune teller waived her hand in a shooing motion, indicating Inga was done and should leave.

As Inga stepped out of the trailer, Katie rushed up the steps. "My turn."

"So, what do you think? Is the Fortune Teller legit?" Violet asked.

"What kind of a question is that? Of course, it's not real. No one can tell another person what will happen in their future," Stephanie said.

"Care to share?" Nora asked.

Inga handed the piece of paper to Violet, who in turn handed it to Stephanie, who in turn handed it to Gwen and lastly to Nora.

"At least it's a good fortune. Let's hope it comes true," Stephanie said.

"Come on, you're not buying into this stuff, are you?" Inga shook her head.

Minutes later, Katie came down the trailer's steps, paper in hand grinning from ear to ear.

Violet practically ran to the steps to be next.

Each romance book club member shared their fortune while the next one took their turn. Being romantics at heart, they were all thrilled to find romance in their fortunes.

They continued strolling leisurely down the other side of the street where the craft brewery tents were located.

Inga spotted a tent with *Nordic Brewing* as the name. She selected it out of the five tents because of her love for all things Nordic and Viking. In fact, the Viking Ship logo caught her eye first. She walked up to the counter to see the menu more closely.

"What can I get you?"

Inga looked up quickly when she heard the strong Norwegian accented English and to her surprise saw almost a '*Thor*' look alike, only his blonde hair was shorter. He could very well be from Viking blood, she thought. *Tall, muscular, with a chiseled face. Have I just died and gone to Valhalla?*

"What can I get you?" he repeated smiling broadly at her.

"What would you suggest?" she managed to get out. "I've never tried your brand before."

"For you lovely lady, I'd suggest the Viking Blonde Ale."

"Sounds absolutely perfect."

He turned his broad toned back toward her stretching the black T-shirt taut against his muscles and filled a plastic souvenir cup with Valhalla printed on one side and a picture of a Viking on the other side.

Inga pulled a five-dollar bill from her purse and set it on the counter. He handed her the cup instead of setting it down and her fingers lightly brushed his in the process. *There it was again.* A shiver of sorts shimmied its way through her body.

"Thank you, hope you enjoy it," he said as he picked up the money to put in the cash register.

"Thanks, I'm sure I will," Inga said while her eyes lingered on this modern-day Viking man. She felt sad that she would most likely not ever see him again. *Oh well, one can only wish.* She turned and walked away spotting her friends up ahead at a different craft brewery tent.

Made in the USA
Monee, IL
24 August 2022

11359082R00042